Jules Verne
THE MYSTERIOUS ISLAND

essay by
Beth Nachison, Ph.D.
Connecticut State University

The Mysterious Island
adaptation by Manning L. Stokes
art by Robert Webb & David Heames
cover by Richard Case

For Classics Illustrated Study Guides
computer recoloring by VanHook Studios
editor: Madeleine Robins
assistant editor: Gregg Sanderson
design: Scott Friedlander

Classics Illustrated: The Mysterious Island © Twin Circle Publishing Co., a division of Frawley Enterprises; licensed to First Classics, Inc. All new material and compilation © 1997 by Acclaim Books, Inc.

Dale-Chall R.L.: 7.5

ISBN 1-57840-033-3

Classics Illustrated® is a registered trademark of the Frawley Corporation.

Acclaim Books, New York, NY
Printed in the United States

STUDY GUIDE

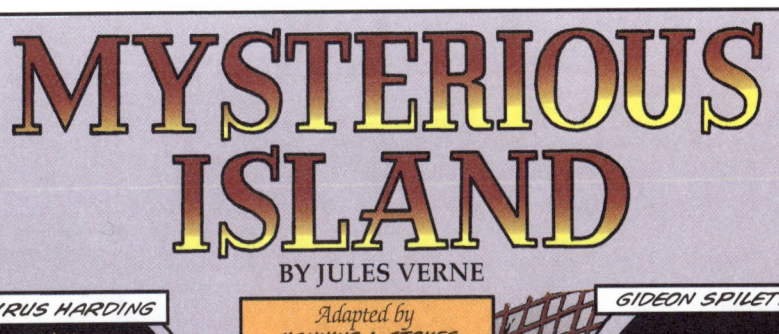

A FEW MINUTES LATER, THE BALLOON AGAIN DIPS...

"CAPTAIN HARDING, WHERE IS HE?"

"HE MUST HAVE FALLEN INTO THE SEA!"

"WE ARE MAROONED. WHERE?..."

"FORWARD. PERHAPS CAPTAIN HARDING HAS BEEN ABLE TO SWIM ASHORE."

"BRRR... IT'S FREEZING!"

THE WEARY HOURS PASS BUT THERE IS NO SIGN OF THEIR LEADER...

"WE'LL FIND THE CAPTAIN YET."

"WE MUST NOT DESPAIR. PERHAPS HE IS WOUNDED AND UNABLE TO REPLY TO OUR CALLS!"

"I MUST FIND THE CAPTAIN... I MUST..."

THE FOLLOWING MORNING, THEY DISCOVER THAT THEY ARE SITUATED ON AN ISLET, SEPARATED FROM THE MAINLAND BY A CHANNEL. TAKING ADVANTAGE OF THE LOW TIDE, THEY CROSS...

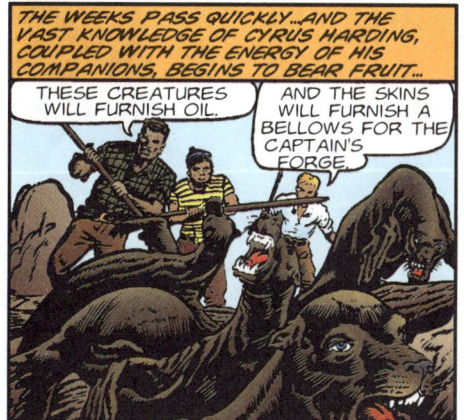

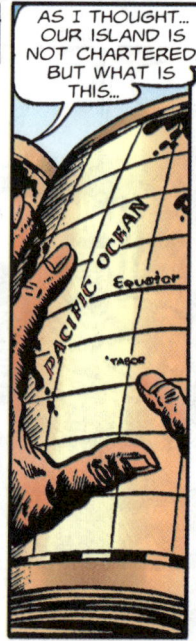

BUT THE LIGHT WASN'T HARDING'S WORK, IT WAS A LENDING HAND FROM THE MYSTERIOUS BENEFACTOR.

LATER AT GRANITE HOUSE, THE CASTAWAY FROM TABOR ISLAND IS CLEANLY SHAVED, LOANED CLOTHING AND GRANTED HIS REQUEST THAT HE MAY LIVE ASIDE FROM THE GROUP, IN SOLITUDE...HE HAS ASSUMED THE WATCH OVER THEIR ANIMAL CORRAL, SPEAKS VERY SELDOM BUT IN HIS RESERVED WAY IS HELPFUL AND NOT UNFRIENDLY...

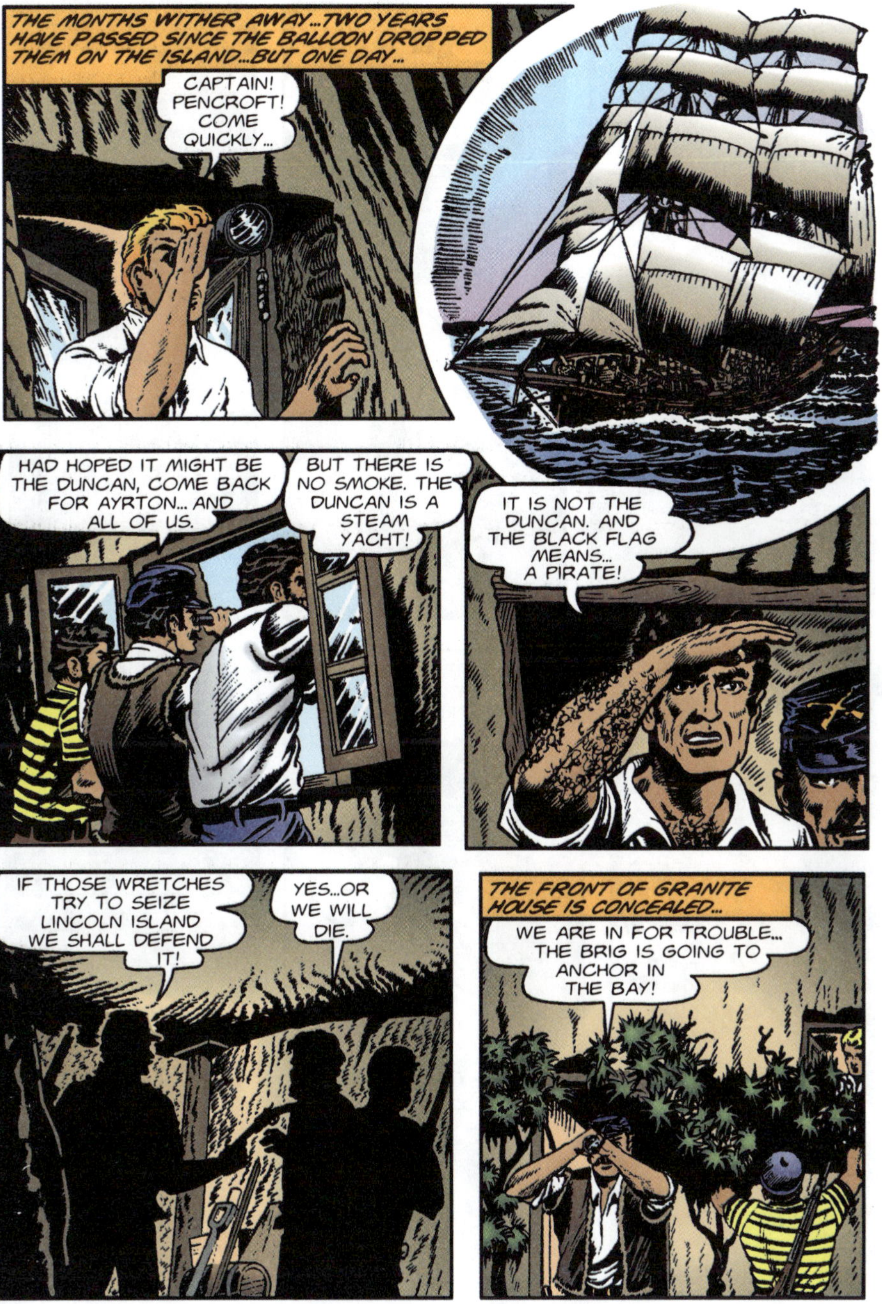

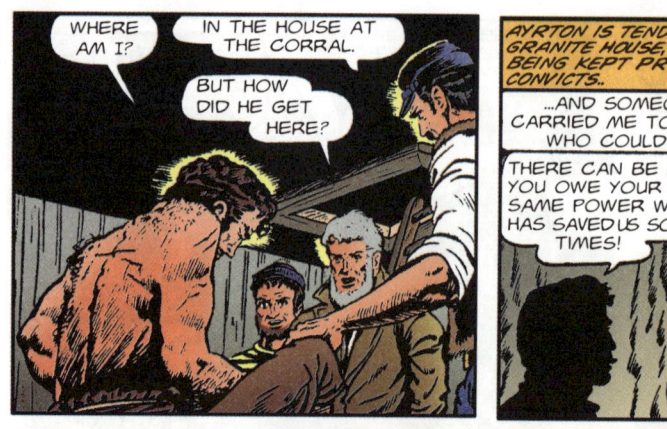

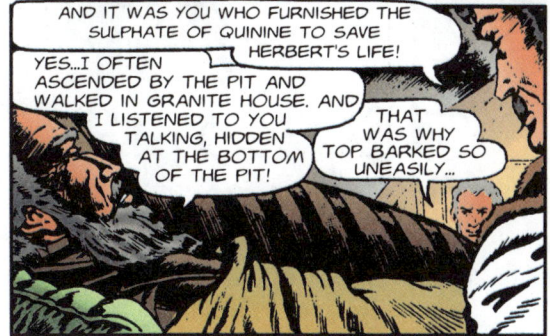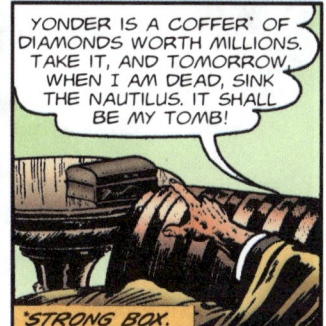

THE MYSTERIOUS ISLAND
JULES VERNE

At the heart of Jules Verne's 1874 novel *The Mysterious Island* is a simple question. If you were stranded on a desert island, how would you survive?

You'd have to find food and water. Could you recognize what's good to eat? You'd have to get shelter from the sun and the weather. Could you build one? You might have to start a fire out of nothing, or protect yourself from storms and dangerous animals, or make your own clothing. You would probably want to be rescued. Would you even be able to figure out where you are?

In *The Mysterious Island*, Jules Verne isn't really interested in man's struggle against nature, or even in man's struggle against human nature. Instead, he provides us with a triumphant vision of man's inevitable triumph *over* nature. Castaways who work together and use all their education and skills for their common good don't have to be at the mercy of the wilderness, he tells us, but can master it, and transform it. Technology and intelligence ensure that humans and civilization, not untamed nature, will prevail.

At least, that is, until Nature bites back. In the end, it seems, the volcano always wins.

The Author

Jules Verne was born in Nantes, on the west coast of France, in 1828. As a boy he was fascinated by the sea and longed to be a sailor. On one occasion he even tried to run away aboard a ship, only to be discovered and brought home at the last minute. In the end it was his younger brother who got to join the Navy, while Jules was sent by his father to study law in Paris. He discovered he liked the literary life better, however; he never attended classes, hung around with other writers in restaurants and cafés and fashionable salons, and learned from older, more successful authors something of the craft and discipline a professional writer required. Young Verne wrote plays, opera libretti, and stories, some of which were actually published, but supported himself as a stockbroker until 1863, when a children's publisher issued his novel *Five Weeks in a Balloon*, an adventurous story about travel around Africa. This was the first of many novels and stories he wrote over forty years: over sixty books in all. A highly successful author from this point on, he lived a prosperous middle-class life, married and had several children

(including a son, Michel, who also became a writer), owned a yacht which he sailed in the Mediterranean, and received public honors from the French government. He died, much respected, in 1905.

A number of Verne's novels are still widely-read and well-loved today: *Journey to the Center of the Earth* (1863), *From the Earth to the Moon* (1865), *Twenty Thousand Leagues Under the Sea* (1870), *Around the World in Eighty Days* (1873), as well as *The Mysterious Island* (1874). In all of these Verne demonstrates his love of travel and his fascination with scientific or technological wonders—the locations are exotic, if not fanciful, and the mechanical marvels frequently on display are often closer to science fiction than to reality. All of these novels are sturdy adventure stories too, filled with optimism and confidence in human ingenuity. But the works of his later years, like those of H.G. Wells and other writers active at the same time, show a darker mood, in which the benevolence of technology and the wisdom of those who use it can no longer be taken for granted. His last major novel, *Master of the World* (1904), features the scientist/inventor Robur, very like the mysterious Nemo of *Twenty Thousand Leagues* and *The Mysterious Island* in some ways, but presented here as a dangerous megalomaniac, in whose hands science has become an uncontrollable weapon. It's not surprising, perhaps, that his later works have not remained as popular as the early ones.

The Characters

Other novelists of Verne's day wrote penetrating studies of character and psychology—Flaubert's *Madame Bovary*, for instance, or Dostoyevsky's *Crime and Punishment*. That wasn't Verne's goal, and that's not why we read him. As *The Mysterious Island* demonstrates, he didn't really care about rounded characters with rich inner lives and complex emotional and psychological states. The characters in this novel are differentiated from each other just enough to keep the reader's attention. They only exist as individuals to the extent that they can advance the plot and give us information and moments of dramatic suspense. They are fictional *types* more than living people. But the choice of types Verne made in populating his novel is interesting, and can tell us a lot about the kind of story he was crafting.

CYRUS HARDING is, from the opening scenes, the dominant member of the group on Lincoln Island. A former officer in the Union Army in the American Civil War, he's brave, decisive, intelligent, a natural leader whom the others all rely upon.

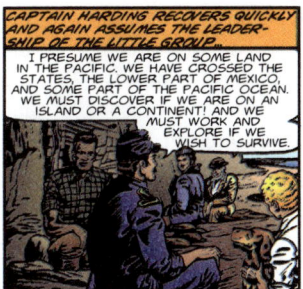

Above all, he is the Engineer—the high priest of high tech. He knows the secrets of machines. He can build them out of virtually nothing, starting from as simple a base as two watch-

Verne on Film

Most of Verne's great novels have been filmed for the movies or TV more than once. The Walt Disney version of *Twenty Thousand Leagues Under the Sea* (1954) is particularly memorable, as is the 1956 film of *Around the World in Eighty Days* with David Niven. Many may also remember the 1961 movie *Mysterious Island*, with lively special effects by Ray Harryhausen, which was very loosely based on this novel.

TV producers as well have been inspired by his works: in the 1980s Michael Palin successfully attempted to imitate Phileas Fogg's 80-day journey around the world, while the adventures of the Nemo's submarine *Nautilus* find an echo in the 1960s series *Voyage to the Bottom of the Sea*, and more recently *Seaquest D.S.V.* Despite their age, Verne's stories have lost none of their ability to capture the imagination.

---

glasses and a dog's steel collar to develop all the essential elements of modern (for the 1870s) industrial technology. He not only builds machines, he knows how to find or create the materials which machines need to run, or which the machines can transform into the good things of civilization.

He's also the group's leader. They were all in the balloon in the first place because he brought them together. When it seemed he was lost at sea, the other castaways despaired, but Harding's recovery quickly gave them hope and purpose, and he set them to work in productive directions. He takes the lead in their extensive explorations of the island. Later, when pirates threaten, he directs their responses. While everyone in the group gets a say in their discussions, Harding generally has the last word.

And more than any of the others, Harding is aware of the continuing mystery of the island and their benefactor, and finally determines to resolve it. His strength holds the others together, and keeps them on course to civilization. When they finally meet their benefactor, the mysterious Captain Nemo, in his submarine *Nautilus*, Harding is the one who has heard of him (from Verne's earlier book!) and he's the one Nemo treats as an equal.

PENCROFT, the other character most fully developed by Verne, is not a leader like Harding, nor is he an educated man. He's a man of the common people, and his major concerns tend to be physical: he's obsessed, for example, with his craving for tobacco, a vice notably lacking in any of the rest. He's impulsive, emotional, preferring action to contemplation. He responds to each new discovery in a simple way: is it dangerous? Can we eat it? (See image on next page). Once assured of survival and his essential comforts, he's content to live as a "colonist" on Lincoln Island, at least

the balloon. He's had little exposure to the world, but he has read a lot, particularly about "natural history." Once they land on the island, it's Herbert, rather than the adults, who can identify all the plants, animals, shellfish, birds, and other things they see, not only by their proper name and species, but also by their useful characteristics. Herbert tells the others how useful or threatening each discovery might be to them, which ones are good to eat, which ones they might easily control, tame, or cultivate, which ones have hidden properties worth knowing about. Every party of castaways needs someone this knowledgeable; in *The Swiss Family Robinson* the second son, Ernest, has a similar broad knowledge of the local flora and fauna.

Herbert's grasp of the natural world is encyclopedic: he's never stumped, and never wrong. He's active and cheerful, always ready to help out in any job that's at hand, and eager to explore, without being headstrong or foolish or disobedient. He's also an innocent whom the adults in the party are determined to protect. That the pirates should shoot *him*, out of all of them, stirs his friends to anger, and the mysterious appearance of the medicine to save him is the most miraculous intervention of their hidden benefactor, even if it's not necessarily the most timely or most important.

until the possibility of rescue presents itself—and even then he foresees a return to the island, as part of a more organized American colony, so he can remain in this perfect place the rest of his days. He lives in the moment, and his dreams for the future revolve largely around a continuation of his present contentment. The arrival of the pirates disturbs him deeply, and after the mysterious destruction of the pirate ship Pencroft is far more anxious than his companions to exterminate the survivors who threaten their continued safety on the island—and it turns out that he's right. As a representative of the working class, Pencroft brings to the group not just his physical power but a practical experience and skill in necessary crafts of daily living, and a wealth of common sense. His expertise as a sailor is unquestioned and invaluable.

HERBERT, the boy, is an orphan and Pencroft's companion before their flight from Richmond in

GIDEON SPILLETT, a reporter, has a few other odd skills to share. He's the closest thing they have to a doctor, and tends the wounded Herbert (though that incident underlines their vulnerability to illness and injury, with no real physician or medical equipment in their colony). More regularly he shows himself a "sportsman"—that is, he's a good hunter, and enthusiastically shoots at anything in sight. His major role in the story, however, is to provide Harding with another educated man to talk to. He's the only one as much at home in the world of ideas as Harding, and they share a paternalistic desire to keep from the others information that could alarm them. The fact that, when the boat *Bonadventure* was nearly lost in the storm, the fire on the island that guided them home and saved them was not lit by Harding, but by some unknown hand, was at first a secret between Harding and Spillett, and only afterwards revealed to the rest. Spillett is always in the thick of the action, frequently contributing ideas or information, but his personality is not clearly drawn, and he has no consistent point of view.

NEB, the former slave, is slavishly devoted to Harding, who freed him. He does the cooking and cleaning at Granite House, with the help of the orangutan Jup. He's regarded by the other "colonists" of Lincoln Island as an equal participant in their community, yet he seldom says much in their discussions, and on the only occasion he has an important job to do on his own, protecting the cultivated plateau against pirates while his companions tend to Herbert in the corral, he fails (though not through any fault of his own). Neb seems to exist in the story mainly as background exotica (despite the long history of French involvement in the Caribbean, and more recent imperialist adventures in Africa, there were relatively few black people in Verne's France in the 1870s, and the French were therefore fascinated with that aspect of American culture), and because *someone* has to be the servant and do the cooking and cleaning.

AYRTON, the castaway of Tabor Island, is the only non-American in the main cast of this book: he was originally a sailor from England, who then spent years as a pirate called "Ben Joyce," based in Australia. Unlike the men of Lincoln Island, Ayrton did not end up on his island as an accidental victim of misfortune. Lord Glenarvon of the *Duncan* deliberately left him there because of his crimes. The island was to be his prison, on which he was to repent, and from which Glenarvon would eventually release him when he had served out a sentence of unspecified length. Abandoned, Ayrton certainly repented. But his decay from civilized to bestial state implies that, for a time, his wicked and animal nature overcame him; alone, exiled from humanity, he lost his own humanity, and gave free reign to all those impulses

> I ATTEMPTED TO STEAL A SHIP, THE DUNCAN, FROM LORD GLENARVAN, MY MASTER IN AUSTRALIA. HOWEVER, BEFORE I MANAGED TO PUT OUT TO SEA WITH MY PIRATE CREW, I WAS DISCOVERED...

Marooned!

Over the years, a lot of real people have found themselves in this predicament. Sailors have been shipwrecked, pilots shot down, travelers lost in unknown parts, and somehow they have to find the means to stay alive, and to return to civilization. It's also a natural set-up for fiction. The most famous example is *Robinson Crusoe*, written by Daniel Defoe in 1719 after he read about the true adventures of the sailor Alexander Selkirk, who was marooned on an island off Chile from 1704 to 1709. In the novel, Robinson Crusoe was shipwrecked on an island with little but his own wits, a few tools, and a Bible. There he lived, not four, but twenty-four years. He spent his days building, farming, contemplating his situation as an exile from the world. Crusoe fought cannibal savages, won the loyalty of the brave Friday, and finally returned home to England, only to discover that, after so many years, it was no longer truly his home after all. Robinson Crusoe's story is an exciting one, but it was also meant to provoke the reader to serious thought about religion, philosophy, and the nature of human communities and human morality. A man who's alone for decades has a *lot* of time to think about things!

Robinson Crusoe inspired a lot of imitators. Most of them didn't have the deeper philosophical concerns of Daniel Defoe and his contemplative hero, and just told lurid action-adventure stories the public eagerly devoured. Variations on the theme of the marooned survivor also appeared. In *The Swiss Family Robinson* (1813) the Swiss author Johann Rudolph Wyss domesticated the scenario—instead of an isolated man alone in the wilderness, he stranded a whole family on an island paradise, ensured their survival was never seriously in danger by providing them with all the necessities from their wrecked ship, and gave them a series of adventures by which each of the young Robinsons could learn the importance of virtue, morality, and obedience to their father. So popular was this book that other writers began to create their own adventures for the Robinsons, which publishers included in Wyss's book as if they were part of the original novel. People couldn't get enough of the shipwrecked family. The Swiss Robinsons were different from Robinson Crusoe and other castaways in another important respect—instead of yearning for a return to civilization, and desperately grasping the first opportunity for it which presented itself, they came to view themselves not as stranded victims of nature, but as active colonists. Father Robinson, in the end, allows some of his family to take ship for Europe, but he and the others voluntarily remain on their island, which had become itself a little outpost of Europe in the wilds.

The Swiss Family Robinson has inspired imitations of its own, a popular Disney movie, and at a more distant remove the 1960s sci-fi series *Lost In Space*, where the family of space-travelers is significantly also called Robinson. And don't forget the 1960s sit-com *Gilligan's Island*, in which a group of castaways with very different talents and characteristics make a home on a deserted isle.

which human society ordinarily restrains and conceals. His return to a human existence after he is brought to Lincoln Island is slow but complete, and his moral regeneration is also complete, as he proves by rejecting the chance to betray his new companions and to rejoin the pirates.

CAPTAIN NEMO was well-known to Verne's readers as the sinister but fascinating central figure of *Twenty Thousand Leagues Under the Sea*, the builder and captain of the magnificent submarine *Nautilus* who harbored a profound distaste for human society. The discovery that he is the mysterious benefactor is the climactic revelation of the novel (although his picture on the first page of the CI adaptation may spoil the surprise a little). The novel is set many years after *Twenty Thousand Leagues*, so Nemo is much older now and all his companions on the submarine have died; but *The Mysterious Island* appeared only four years after the earlier book, so Verne's readers would have been delighted that it turned out to be a kind of sequel. We learn Nemo's true history as an Indian Prince, educated in Europe, who had unsuccessfully rebelled against British rule over his homeland and fled to the bottom of the sea rather than submit to it any longer. We learn also that he's dying—that's the only reason he finally reveals himself. For anyone familiar with his earlier adventure, it's a sad moment indeed when he dies, and following his instructions Cyrus Harding sinks the *Nautilus* for good. His hand reaches out from beyond the grave, however: it's thanks to his actions that the others are finally rescued just in time after the destruction of their island.

The Plot

Adventures and Invention

The Mysterious Island opens in the middle of action. Four men, a boy, and a dog, unwillingly held in the Confederate capital of Richmond, Virginia in the waning days of the Civil War in 1865, have made off with a Confederate balloon in hopes of escaping to freedom and the north. Unfortunately, their timing is rotten. They fly straight into a hurricane of monstrous proportions which blows them clear to the South Pacific and strands them there. As their balloon slowly deflates, they sink toward the sea, and to avoid being ditched in the middle of the ocean they have to throw overboard everything they possess. To get a little more lift they even cut off the balloon's basket, which leaves them clinging to the netting. Finally, when it seems they're doomed, a wave carries off Cyrus Harding and his faithful dog Top, which allows the balloon to rise above the water for a last crucial few

THE BALLOON SUDDENLY DIPS AND...

minutes and to deposit the remaining passengers on an island—an unknown island, uninhabited, in the middle of nowhere. Bereft without Harding, they search for him or his remains without success, and make a poor meal of raw shellfish. They have only one precious match left to make a fire to warm their rocky shelter. Soon another storm blows up. The dog Top appears and leads them to Harding, who is lying unconscious above the beach. How did he get there? How did Top find them? They don't know, and neither does Harding when he wakes up. On their return to their first camp, they find disaster has struck: the waves have entered, and put out their fire! How can they possibly survive without it?

Only Harding refuses to despair. *He* can make fire for them, by taking apart two watches and focusing sunlight through the glass covers. From that little miracle of applied science, neither Verne nor the castaways look back. They *will* survive, and master the island fate has cast them onto. Ultimately they will leave it again to rejoin the civilized world. Ingenuity, courage, luck, and the occasional intervention of an unknown hand make a fortunate outcome probable, if they manage to overcome each new danger as well as they did that first one.

In the CI adaptation of *The Mysterious Island* we see at least sketchily all the major adventures and mysteries of the original novel. But the scenes of most intense action, from the discovery of Ayrton on the neighboring Tabor Island to the final cataclysm which completely destroys the island, take up altogether only about half of Verne's expansive narrative. The rest is occupied with matters less obviously dramatic, but equally thrilling in Verne's eyes, and in those of many readers—the exploration of the island, the discovery and naming of all its parts and resources, and the castaways' gradual mastering of their physical environment. At first desperate, cold, hungry, at the mercy of the wind and rain and wild animals, they become a prosperous little community with roads, agriculture, industry, and all the comforts of civilized life—even an elevator and a telegraph, both powerful symbols of modernity to Verne's original audience in the 1870s.

Verne describes the geography of Lincoln Island in loving detail. As in other popular books he wrote, like *Twenty Thousand Leagues Under the Sea* and *Around the World in 80 Days*, the travelogue of sights and examples of exotic local color are presented as interesting in their own right. Even more exciting, however, are the technological marvels which flow from the fertile mind and clever hands of Cyrus Harding and his assistants. In *Twenty Thousand Leagues* Verne was inventing futuristic machinery his readers could never have encountered in reality—though technology has since made them commonplace, wonders such as the submarine *Nautilus*, the diving suits, the air conditioning, the electric lights were all beyond the scope of existing technology in the 1860s. In *The Mysterious Island*, however, Verne largely confined himself to practical, everyday machinery, and the marvel was to see it created literally from nothing. Modern life here bootstraps itself out of the wilderness, and Verne invites the readers to share the secrets.

Do you want to make bricks and pottery? Verne tells us how. Want to know how to calculate the latitude and longitude of a place? Verne describes the procedure in detail. How about making iron from raw ore? We learn about it here. The basics of industrial chemistry? Cyrus Harding knows all about making and using potash, sulfuric acid, azootic acid, and other useful substances, and makes sure his companions and the reader do too. The elevator to Granite House and the mill which makes the felt for their clothing run on water power, provided by the lake. The telegraph between Granite House and the corral requires both wire to carry the signal, which we witness being manufactured, and electric power to run, therefore a chemical battery whose construction we are also shown. There are many other examples, which may seem like digressions from the action, but are in fact central to Verne's plan for the novel. It's not just an adventure story, but also a way for readers to learn some of the fundamental elements of industrial technology. Verne finds modern technology exciting and full of promise, and he goes to pains to de-mystify it and show its benefits to the little colony.

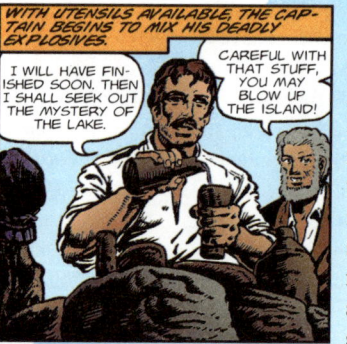

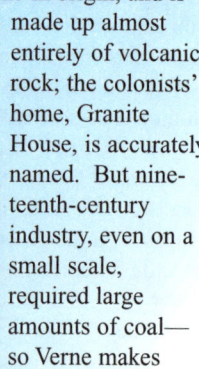

The ease with which Verne's stranded travelers succeed in recreating industrial technology, of course, isn't wholly plausible. Like other authors, Verne used artistic license to provide his characters with whatever natural resources and obstacles his story required, without much regard for real-world probability. Lincoln Island, like Hawaii and a number of other Pacific islands, is volcanic in origin, and is made up almost entirely of volcanic rock; the colonists' home, Granite House, is accurately named. But nineteenth-century industry, even on a small scale, required large amounts of coal—so Verne makes sure there are rich deposits of it on the island, easily mined. Today, coal is known to be a fossil fuel, the remains of forests hundred of millions of years old, and couldn't possibly have formed under the geological conditions Verne had already described. No matter; the story is more important than such a detail.

In depositing plants and animals on the islands Verne is even less hampered by "reality." He mingles the flora and fauna of Asia, Australia, North and South America, Europe, and the Pacific with free abandon. Koalas and kangaroos share meadows and forests with rabbits, peccaries, capybaras, jaguars, orangutans, and wild sheep; birch and sugar maples grow alongside Australian eucalyptus and New Zealand kauri, and the bird population is equally an ecologist's nightmare. The only governing principle seems to be, the more exotic the better. That such a mingling of species could never have occurred in nature in no way makes the story less credible, and only heightens the mystery for readers who notice it.

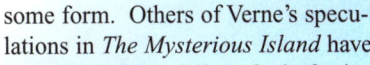

Verne was interested in science as well as technology, and occasionally allows his characters, particularly Harding, to muse upon more abstract questions. Harding is convinced, for instance, that water is the fuel of the future: broken down by electricity into hydrogen and oxygen, it will replace coal to run furnaces, provide heat and light, and supply all the energy needs of humanity after humanity has exhausted all its sources of coal (Book II, Chapter 11). Although Verne's imagery is bound to his time, the idea of water as a cheap, clean, and inexhaustible fuel is still attractive, and researchers are working on ways to achieve it in some form. Others of Verne's speculations in *The Mysterious Island* have fallen afoul of scientific developments in the generations since he wrote, and sound quaint today. Speaking through Harding, he proposes that the continents aren't fixed in place, which was indeed a revolutionary idea a century before the theory of plate tectonics was accepted by scientists to explain their movements; but he goes on from there to claim that coral reefs and islands are the seeds of new continents which Nature is constructing in preparation for the time when the earth grows cold, the temperate zones become uninhabitable, and more living space for the world's plants and animals is required in the tropics (Book 1, Chapter 22). It's unclear whether Verne meant us to take this absolutely seriously, but it's certainly a startling notion.

Towards the end of the novel, drama takes a wild spin into melodrama: the final third of the book features the arrival and destruction of pirates, the shooting of Herbert, the revelation and death of Captain Nemo, and finally the destruction of Lincoln Island itself, blown to smithereens by the volcano. (See image on previous page). Technology does have limits after all; for all their ingenuity, the colonists can't save themselves from the fury of Nature unleashed. As hard as they work to finish the ship for their escape, they can't finish it fast enough—the night before they mean to launch it, the island explodes and destroys it, along with everything else. Our castaways are left even worse off than they were at the outset, clinging not to a large and fertile island but to a barren scrap of rock, doomed to certain death, when the long-hoped-for rescue-ship arrives just in the nick of time to carry them home to safety. Only in a novel do we look for this kind of coincidence! As interested as Verne was in science and machines, he was ultimately more interested in telling a thrilling story. The end of *The Mysterious Island* is a real nail-biter.

Themes

A Tale of Imperialism

Jules Verne lived in an era intoxicated by the idea of Progress. It was assumed the future was bound to be more glorious than the past: old, unsatisfactory political systems were giving way to improved modern governments; agriculture was more productive than ever before, and so was industry. Machines were growing more sophisticated and complex, new inventions every year performed wonders that previous generations could barely dream of, and imagination was the only limit to what might be developed in years to come. Already railroads and steamships could carry goods and people at incredible speeds across vast distances.

The completion of the railroad across the United States which connected an entire continent from ocean to ocean was an amazing feat which inspired Verne to write *Around the World in 80 Days*. The telegraph likewise made rapid communication across vast distances possible for the first time in human history, and at the time of *The Mysterious Island* inventors were already racing to develop a working telephone, which Alexander Graham Bell achieved two years later in 1876.

Many other things we take for granted today excited the public imagination in the mid-nineteenth century, and had a direct impact on the quality of daily life. The sewing machine, the bicycle, the elevator were all important symbols of modernity and convenience, and had an enormous impact on society—the bicycle, for instance, made it possible for people to live a great distance from where they worked, which contributed to the emergence of residential suburbs, while without the elevator, no one would ever have thought of building a skyscraper. Chemical dyes introduced in the 1850s made the world a more colorful place—although it's hard to imagine from black and white photographs, clothing and furniture were as garish in the 1860s as in the 1960s! People couldn't get enough of new-and-improved. They assumed that new *was* improved. They had a boundless confidence in their own ability to make a better world for themselves. Verne shared that confidence.

But Progress also had a darker side. The same technology which made steamships and canned food possible created more advanced military hardware, which made war both easier and deadlier. Railroads carried troops and guns as easily as tourists; the brutal campaigns of the American Civil War and the German siege of Paris in 1871 gave a terrible preview of the wars of the future. The manufactured goods which made middle-class life so pleasant were produced by an army of workers who slaved away in mines and factories and sweatshops, invisible in their desperate poverty, filth, and hunger, never able to benefit from the fruit of their own labors. The idea of Progress underlay the revolutionary vision of Karl Marx, who couldn't imagine the exploited poor would passively accept their fate forever. Wouldn't the better world of the future, he suggested, be better for everyone? Social and political reform were much on people's mind in the mid-nineteenth century. France had four revolutions within Verne's lifetime. This was also the great age of Imperialism, when western powers competed with each other to take over as much of the world as they could. In the United States, the Indian Wars began in earnest as soon as the dust had settled from the Civil War, and by the end of the century Americans had begun to reach beyond the continental boundaries to seize Cuba and the Philippines, while already American businessmen had overthrown the native monarchy of Hawaii and replaced it with a puppet government more to their liking. The British had taken control of India, depriving its own rulers of all independence and making Queen Victoria an Empress, while British emigrants looking for a new life ballooned the population of colonial settlements in Australia and South Africa: it was said accurately that "the Sun never sets on the British Empire." The King of Siam barely managed to retain his nation's independence while the rest of Indochina fell into the hands of the French. Many European states, with the US as a latecomer, carved out "spheres of influence" in China, much to the dismay of the Chinese who couldn't put up any effective resistance. And in Africa the French and British and other European powers did not put up even a show of working through or with the Africans but simply claimed vast lands for themselves to do with as they pleased, slicing up the continent in treaties no African ever saw.

This kind of bold-faced land-grabbing, so repulsive to us, wasn't something anyone at the time was ashamed about. On the contrary, nations were proud of their successes at empire-building, for it too was clear evidence of Progress. Europeans, and their descendants in places like North America and Australia, took it for granted that European civilization, values, habits and culture were superior to everyone else's. Those who didn't share them were at best barbarians, at worst savages. Europeans had a duty to bestow on the rest of the world the blessings of civilization, to educate and protect inferior peoples from their own savagery; and while so doing it was their right to establish dominion over the "uncivilized" lands of others and to use their resources for civilized purposes. Missionaries poured out of Europe to bring Christianity to the heathen. Businessmen scoped out the natural resources and mineral wealth of "savage" continents and exploited them ruthlessly. Governments supported them as a point of national pride, and threw their weight around like schoolyard bullies. Rudyard Kipling wrote, possibly ironically, of the "White Man's Burden." Today we recognize it as a racist ideal, but to the mind of the nineteenth-century European or American it was natural to view peoples and cultures along the linear track of Progress just as they saw machines, with the primitive and inferior inevitably giving way before the improved and superior. The assumption of their own superiority empowered Europeans to act, and few questioned it.

Viewed against this background, *The Mysterious Island* takes on a somewhat different color. Verne fully endorses the sentiments of his age. His enthusiasm for technology is obvious. It's largely thanks to the engineering skill of Cyrus Harding in developing small but effective industry on the island that the castaways can rise above mere survival to build a "colony," an outpost of Euro-American civilization in their new land. To a reader accustomed to late twentieth-century environmentalism, the admiring descriptions of industrial chemistry Verne provides us are startling, but he subscribes wholeheartedly to the attitude expressed in the 1950s slogan, "Better living through chemistry." And, even "knowing better," how many of us would voluntarily go without the products of industry that fill our lives?

Cyrus Harding, pointing to the iron, coal, and other minerals of Lincoln Island, says roundly, "Nature gives us these things. It is our business to make a right use of them" (Book 1, Chapter 12). That says it all. Everything found on the island

> AND HERE IS THE GREATEST TREASURE OF ALL!

has been placed there for human exploitation. The only moral choice is the best way to use the resources.

And if this is true for the rocks and clay, it's even more so for the living things of the island. It's not much of an exaggeration to say that the colonists will kill anything that moves, and take pleasure in it. What a slaughter they make of their birds and animals! True, they have to hunt to eat. But in just a few weeks one spring they shoot down agouties, kangaroos, capybaras, pigeons, wild ducks, and snipes, and catch rabbits and peccaries with their traps and snares. The quantity of meat for five people and one dog is astounding, and continuously replenished. Gideon Spillett is a particularly good "sportsman," bringing down game with arrows, guns, even thrown rocks. With regard to the non-edible creatures that share the island, they are even more ruthless. Wild sheep and onagers are domesticated for wool and labor. With the jaguars they are at open war. Their intention, bluntly stated, is to make them extinct on the island. Though they see that as a desirable goal, today we can't read that passage without a shudder.

And what of the orangutans? They were a little-known and exotic animal to the nineteenth-century public. Edgar Allan Poe featured a captive one in "The Murders in the Rue Morgue." Verne's readers (and possibly Verne himself) would not have known they are solitary animals which never live in troops like the one which invades Granite House. The reaction of the returning men, though, is telling. They see the orangutans as a menace to everything they have, as dangerous as the jaguars, and treat them as such. Of the apes, Jup is the sole survivor of the battle for Granite House. And Jup they make their servant. They dress him in clothing, train him to wait on the table and run errands and help Neb in the kitchen, teach him to smoke Pencroft's pipe. It doesn't stretch the imagination far to see in Jup the "primitive" peoples of Africa, India, Australia, and elsewhere, treated at worst to outright extermination as they were driven from their homes and deprived of land and livelihood and future along with their independence, at best viewed with a condescending paternalism as servants and flunkies who can only ape the civilization of their betters. In the desperate scramble of the final volcanic cataclysm, none of the colonists thinks to save Jup, though he fought bravely alongside them against attacking foxes, and they all owe their lives to his loyalty and intelligence during the pirate invasion; unlike Top, the faithful dog they brought with them from America, Jup dies ignored and forgotten with the donkeys and fowl and other tame beasts.

It's unlikely that Verne deliberately wrote *The Mysterious Island* as a parable of imperialism. But its echoes resonate throughout the novel, often in disturbing ways. It's a reminder how deeply embedded a writer is in the culture and unspoken assumptions of his own society, and how different the subtext of a work of fiction might be, viewed from a century's distance, from the author's conscious intentions when he wrote.

Study Questions

- Each of the castaways contributes talents to the group. Does Verne consider any of these contributions more important than others? Why?
- Why has Verne, a Frenchman, made all his main characters here American? Do they have any characteristics his audience would have perceived as more "American" than "European"?
- What is the significance of the group's choice to consider themselves "colonists" rather than "castaways"? How does the label help define their relationship with their island?
- What is the group's attitude toward the island? How do they treat its other inhabitants? Why?
- What steps do the characters take to recreate civilization on the island? Which steps seem the most important? How do they define civilization? Do the achieve it?
- How realistic is the technology Verne allows his characters? What do you think are the most important or useful things they make? How many of these things are really essential for their survival, and how many are just really exciting gizmos?
- Why do the colonists make Jup part of their group? Is Jup closer in status to Top or to Neb? Would this question have been as disturbing to Verne's original audience as it might be today?
- Why did Ayrton, surviving alone on Tabor Island, degenerate into a beast? Aside from solitude, what makes his situation different from those of the group on Lincoln Island?
- Why are there no women in the book?
- Do you think the group could have survived without their "mysterious benefactor"? Why is Nemo in this book at all?
- What's Verne's reason for blowing up the island at the end? How (if at all) does this final act of Nature change our perceptions of the possibilities of technology to govern Nature? Can Nature be civilized?

About the Essayist:

Beth Nachison is an Assistant Professor in the History Department at Connecticut State University, where she specializes in the history of modern France. She holds a B.A. from Dartmouth College and an M.A. and Ph.D. from the University of Iowa.